PEQUEÑOS DEPORTISTAS

SPORTS FOR SPROUTS

GIMNASIA

GYMNASTICS

Holly Karapetkova

ROURKE PUBLISHING

Vero Beach, Florida 32964

© 2010 Rourke Publishing LLC

All rights reserved. No part of this book may be reproduced or utilized in any form or by any means, electronic or mechanical including photocopying, recording, or by any information storage and retrieval system without permission in writing from the publisher.

www.rourkepublishing.com

Photo credits: All photography by Renee Brady for Blue Door Publishing, except Cover © Wendy Nero; Title Page © Wendy Nero, Crystal Kirk, Leah-Anne Thompson, vnosokin, Gerville Hall, Rob Marmion; Page 8 © © Vyacheslav Osokin; Page 12 © Robert J. Daveant; Page 14 © Tony Wear; Sidebar Silhouettes © Sarah Nicholl

Editor: Meg Greve

Cover and page design by Nicola Stratford, Blue Door Publishing
Bilingual editorial services by Cambridge BrickHouse, Inc.   www.cambridgebh.com

Acknowledgements: Thank you to *Tumbleweeds* (www.tumbleweedsgym.net), Melbourne, Florida, for their assistance on this project

Library of Congress Cataloging-in-Publication Data

Karapetkova, Holly.
  Gymnastics / Holly Karapetkova.
    p. cm. -- (Sports for sprouts)
  ISBN 978-1-60694-325-0 (hard cover)
  ISBN 978-1-60694-825-5 (soft cover)
  ISBN 978-1-60694-566-7 (bilingual)
  1. Gymnastics--Juvenile literature. I. Title.
  GV461.3.K37 2010
  796.44--dc22
                                            2009002258

Printed in the USA

CG/CG

www.rourkepublishing.com - rourke@rourkepublishing.com
Post Office Box 643328 Vero Beach, Florida 32964

Soy una gimnasta.

I am a gymnast.

3

Durante mi clase de gimnasia, llevo una **malla**.

At my gymnastics class, I wear a **leotard**.

5

Estiramos nuestros brazos y piernas.

We stretch our arms and legs.

8

Hacemos maromas sobre la colchoneta.

We tumble on the mats.

Damos volteretas.

We do somersaults.

Caminamos sobre la barra de equilibrio. ¡No te caigas!

We walk on the balance beam. Don't fall!

Damos vueltas en las barras.

We flip around the bars.

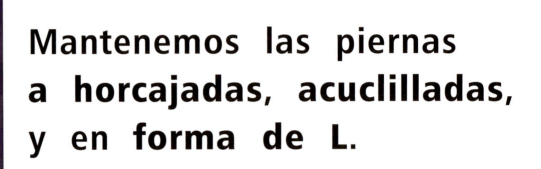

Mantenemos las piernas a **horcajadas**, **acuclilladas**, y en **forma de L**.

We hold our legs in **straddles**, **tucks**, and **pikes**.

17

Es divertido usar el **minitrampolín** para saltar muy alto.

It's fun to use the **minitrampoline** to jump high.

19

Nos animamos unos a otros. ¡Siempre damos el máximo!

We cheer for each other. We always try our best!

Glosario / Glossary

acuclilladas: En esta posición, las piernas de la gimnasta se mantienen recogidas.
tuck (TUK): In a tuck, the gymnast keeps the legs close to the body.

a horcajadas: En esta posición, las piernas de la gimnasta se abren hacia los lados.
straddles (STRAD-uhlz): In a straddle, the gymnast's legs spread wide out to either side.

forma de L: En esta posición, la gimnasta mantiene las piernas extendidas formando una L.
pikes (PIKES): In a pike, the gymnast keeps the legs straight forming an L.

malla: Una malla es una prenda pegada al cuerpo que lo cubre desde los hombros hasta las caderas. Las bailarinas y gimnastas usan mallas.

leotard (LEE-uh-tard): A leotard is a tight piece of clothing that covers the body from the shoulders to the thighs. Dancers and gymnasts wear leotards.

minitrampolín: Un minitrampolín es un equipo de ejercicio hecho de una lona fuerte sujetada a un armazón por resortes. Los gimnastas pueden brincar muy alto en él.

minitrampoline (MIN-eetram-puh-LEEN): A minitrampoline is a piece of exercise equipment made of strong canvas attached to a frame with springs. It allows gymnasts to bounce up high.

volteretas: En una voltereta, la cabeza se coloca en el piso y el cuerpo rota sobre la cabeza. Las volteretas también se llaman vueltas de carnero.

somersaults (SUHM-ur-sawlts): Somersaults are rolls where the head goes down on the ground and the body turns over the head. Another word for somersaults is forward rolls.

23

Índice / Index

Visita estas páginas en Internet / Websites to Visit

www.usa-gymnastics.org
www.fig-gymnastics.com
www.gymnasticszone.com

Sobre la autora / About the Author

A Holly Karapetkova, Ph.D., le encanta escribir libros y poemas para niños y adultos. Ella da clases en la Universidad de Marymount y vive en la zona de Washington, D.C., con su hijo K.J. y sus dos perros, Muffy y Attila.

Holly Karapetkova, Ph.D., loves writing books and poems for kids and adults. She teaches at Marymount University and lives in the Washington, D.C., area with her husband, her son K.J., and her two dogs, Muffy and Attila.